The World Is A Dark And Lovely Place
Carol Meiyin

The world is a dark and lovely place
ISBN: 978-967-0730-44-8

Published by The Inspiration Hub

Printed in Malaysia.
First Printing, 2019

Dedication

For Papa, Mama, Ben and Peter,
and for you too dear reader,

This book is for you.

Contents

Dear reader,

Hi! I'm Carol Meiyin.

Just in case you are confused with the name on this book cover, just know that I had to put my full name there for both my parents' sake. Without them, I'm a total nobody. God bless them.

These are my collection of poems that I have written ever since I was 19. The first poem I wrote was *The Old Oak Tree*. I remember those as one of my most inspiring times because I went on to write *The World Is A Dark And Lovely Place*, which inspired the title of this poetry book, and I continued it with *The Rainbow's End* and *Rain*, both of which got published in *The Star* newspaper in the year 2008. (Yes, I'm that ancient!) The rest is history.

This book was originally published as a poetry chapbook on sites such as Amazon, Kobo and various other platforms, totalling only 19 on the 3rd July 2018. However, due to circumstances involving printing an actual physical book, I was told that it is better to have more poems for more volume in a book. Hence, this book in your hands is the result of that, so to my original poetry chapbook readers, you have more poems to read! (Yay?)

Do drop me an honest review at Goodreads or anywhere online, even brickbats are truly welcome. So that if I ever have my next poetry collection, I would know what areas to improve.

In all the inky words spilled on pages of books, there would be no writers if the world has no readers. Thank you for your precious time in reading this book.

Love books well, and they will love you well.

With love from the very bottom of my heart,
Carol Meiyin

I hear my happy thoughts sing,
of shapes and sounds the April rain brings.

The World Is A Dark And Lovely Place

If somehow I could find the places,
beyond those books I read,
and catch fickle rainbows by the tail,
A lover's breath that stays,
on wintry window panes,

If somehow I could hear,
the happy talk of the brook,
and see where those lovely thoughts run,
Then I could remember,
how this changing world looks,

Sundusts that glow bright,
under the dusty morning light,
Stormy purple clouds,
on rainy marvellous nights,

Then perhaps somehow somewhere,
sometime in the evening,
When I feel my tall shadow shaking,
and my heart starts beating,
Shall I go where the paths disappear?

Though I do not know where I'll be,
there will always be dreams,
Someday I'll be home again,
Once I know where I am,
the world is a dark and lovely place.

The Old Oak Tree

The old oak tree grew at the edge,
of an orchard where little ones play,
and there lived a mage,
who hears trees on a windy day,

Rushing wind rustles leaves,
on that one day brilliant and bright,
With amber gold autumn grandeur on display,
singing tuneful songs delightfully light and gay,
Apple trees trilling events as mysterious as night,
of love found and lost last May,

But the wise oak tree stood stiff and straight,
then shook its great leafy crown silently in retreat,
bowing low reverently in sorrow,
Memories of Tuesdays, of late long afternoons,
where lovers meet like there's no tomorrow,

A shadow passes, fast and certain,
passing apple trees chirping news of a coming mage,
to the old oak tree in crumpled heap the Master lay,
shades of sunlight showing his face lifeless that day,
A still breeze, the trees hush, huddling closer in a curtain,
trying to hear what the young man had to say,

'The other side of this world I was,
where skies are cloudless and dusks are endless,
In those towns and cities, treeless and friendless I last,
till I could no more when a quiet breeze blows in doubt,
and left me a sore stinging mark,

Passing a withered hawthorn who told a woeful tale of her without,
shoes to run about,
shoes to tread perilous roads at dark',

It seemed many ages past, a day in his sodden memory,
when the oak tree felt a tug in his wooden heart,
feeling gentle arms halfway round his trunk,

'Thou art who, this slender wee might,
hugging hale and hearty me so tight.'
'Oh sir, I am but a midget,
just a lonely wench in your sight',
For the Master, the tree was glad in his part,

Rushing wind rustles leaves,
on that one day gloomy and dim,
A crashing gale, a wailing thunderous storm,
singing tearful songs dismal and grey,
Apple trees clamouring for cover, murmuring in dismay,
of love lost forever last May,

For their Master still and unmoving, perished at waste,
of weariness his energy spent,
beside the cracked old oak tree split into two,
his life's journey was at an end,

A long silence reverberating,
a memory everlasting,
in that pale lifeless heart of wood,
forever dwelling on those lifelong remembered words,
'We will always be together for good'.

The Rainbow's End

I hear my happy thoughts sing,
of shapes and sounds the April rain brings,
To faraway yellow hills I will go,
to seek the throbbing rainbow's end.

I danced along the unseen track,
The path that leads to once spoken dreams,
For these thundering dreams I will keep,
till at the last turning we shall meet.

At the beating of the greying rain,
I will find my home again,
In the depths of this world,
I will find my rainbow's end.

I could touch the whisper of the grass,
when the wind breathes.

Rain

I could see the nimble swallows glide,
reaching pretty clouds that swirl and slide,
When they are tired and weary,
in my secret backyard they go to hide.

I could touch the whisper of the grass,
when the wind breathes,
the sombre murmur of the woods, the bending of trees,
the sound of leaves in the swaying breeze.

I could feel the rhythm grow,
the music that pours in the driving storm,
thinking heartfelt deeds that make one glow,
and lovely thoughts that keep one warm.

I could hear the lazing dull frogs sing,
a sad funny lullaby in between,
the angry bang of thunder once lightning moves,
the thrashing noise of rain on roofs.

I could reach far from where I've been,
further than the winding steady road that goes,
but I would rather leave my heart at home,
when the dear rain falls.

Untitled

I hope the rain comes,
in the slumbering of night,
knocking my window.

I hope that dreams come,
while I am in bed asleep,
hugging my pillow.

The thunder rumbles,
the curtains, the breeze whispers,
my name in the dark.

While the cool wind blows,
it called me up from darkness,
till the night is up.

Wonder what it said,
and then the sun comes out light,
I awoke, troubled.

It did say something,
the breeze that whispers my name,
coolly in the dark.

But what it did say,
I could not remember, but
it stayed in my heart.

My Little Butterfly

Dear little one,
Do never quit flitting around me,
your smiles let me catch them now,
Do work your chubby arms like an aeroplane.

Then, like an artful, charming butterfly,
winking atop the plush sofa down,
Your laughter etched in my heart,
then you fell and stumbled, climbing your way up.

I held you, my dear precious angel,
Your chuckles a silence,
your tears I hold them,
I ache inside a moment.

Were you hurt, my lovely, handsome butterfly?
Let me hold you a moment more,
and tickle your nose and funny bone,
your giggles once more in my heart.

You want something fancy and colourful?
Let's go look for a true little butterfly,
One that flits and fly real sly,
Just like you, my beloved child,

My little butterfly.

She longed to go where the people go,
and breathe the air she knew once more.

Drowning

In wakeful moments of plenty,
deep dark the dream comes,
I drowned, was cold and weary,
and all the time I woke numb,
When someone calls my name,
and all seems to be the same.

The sea shows deep my fear,
though I lie when cruel words fall,
They shine inside of me when I am here,
The sea, the waters I hear them call,
When it thunders and waters rise,
a part of me struggles and dies.

Every time I am awake,
I pray for arms to grab my waist,
When floods set in and a large wave breaks,
I hear the sound my worried heart makes,
My footsteps falter at the edge of shore,
but the waves retreat, a foe no more.

Now when I thrash about in my dreams,
my mind sees a brief respite,
The waves retreat, my pride redeemed,
and all is clear and bright,
When someone calls my name,
I could as yet call out the same.

A Memory

Could not get up,
when darkness fades,
to light the morning sky,
A brand new day,
it calls my heart.

But could not stir,
my hands they're cold,
my feet, they're faint,
Could not work myself,
from where I am,
my name it called.

Last night so dark,
my soul weightless roams,
It goes again,
against my will,
to where you are.

What you said,
and what last you did,
The way you turned,
your head this way and that,
and laughed...and laughed,
when I said "We're too far...from shore".

"Not to worry", you whispered,
"I'll bring you home safe",
Before the wave overtook us,
and swallowed my might,
Against my will,
by chance woke up,

Alone.

The Hearkened Heart

She could not forget those behind bolted doors,
(It was hard and heartless without those behind bolted doors),
She had heard the pitter-patter and the quiet footsteps,
of time that robbed and stole endless days of fun,
It was the one treasure and unseen barrier,
she could not walk through the open doors,
'Memories will float like dusty leaves,
on the windy way where paths made now were seldom warm'.

She longed to go where the people go,
and breathe the air she knew once more,
Over far mountains there drifts her soul,
to feel the words her ears have heard,
and echoes of someone something dear,
Hot fingers touching the solemn cold wind,
the strange music of the trees whispering,
'He was come, he was come'.

The unbreaker had a quiver of listened dreams,
He took an arrow and with his bow of heartened understanding,
shot it at the unbroken door; smashed, splintered the door to shatters,
The wondrous crash it was! Glorious and mighty!
till it shook this place of many moons,
with ground-breaking earthquake, and the roaring of seas,
he rendered the said door to pieces,
Shaken, she stood thunderstruck and amazed,

Hearing the unbreaker murmur 'But do what you can',
and left her thinking in her lost world of many moons,
'I'll be all right', thought she at last,
her hearkened heart beating fast,
she walked towards the open door.

In the loveliest reverie I was walking by,
Your voice I hear low and calling.

A Thousand More Miles To Go

Why do I hear these things,
coming from the wells of my heart,
I'm not easily peeved,
but my feelings hot,

I have many more miles to go,
words to say, things to do,
Dreams to live, if I could,
a life I'm in, without You,

Running always running this present day,
Rushing always rushing, till one day I pay,
I took no heed of what others had to say,
I treat as if You were always away,

Every day it was the same,
I go through all the mundane,
Sometimes I wonder whether life could be even more,
but never once I stopped to look outside the door,

Then one day I took a trip in my dreams,
over vast sunny fields and streams,
A great measureless distance,
in this journey of a thousand million miles,

And You spoke to me, You said,
The world will live in less agony,
if I would stop in a bit, and take heed,
of what others had to say,

Though life is a mystery,
and sometimes, I wonder where I'll be,
There are friends and family,
So for now, I'll let them be my priority,

Till then, a thousand more miles to go each time I stop,
A kind deed always to do for each time I've got,
and though I have many more words to say, and things to do,
I will always ponder and look outside the door,

For finding You now,
will always be my final destination,
For this life has always been about,

You.

Trust Not Your Broken Heart

Trust no one, not even yourself,
Trust not your deceitful heart,
Neither trust your confused mind,
Especially with others,
do not trust your anger at all times,
For words cut deeper than wounds,
both sides might hurt and never return.

Life can be a lie,
Some things might be untrue,
Believe not your naked eye,
nor what you believe to be true,
Do not even trust those whom you trust,
For all will fail, for all will fall,
Let all be warned, caution henceforth.

In God alone let us trust,
We are like a broken vase,
An empty urn He fills us full,
All creatures both great and small,
He watered this fallen world whole,
through the tiny crack which made a hole,
Underground flowers, shrubs start to grow.

Be happy, thankful and glad in Him,
when mere words stab and break you,
and your heart is crushed and bleeding blue,
You know He is entirely true,
because He is deeply there for you,
Therefore trust not your broken heart,
but in He who thought of you,

In He who loves you.

On My Way Home

In the loveliest reverie I was walking by,
Your voice I hear low and calling,
My name the trees echo and sigh,
the waning yellow mountains sprawling,

The birds flutter and flew, gaily,
riding waves in the purring wind,
I sing to heart a happy song, daily,
I feel Your words, how those times begin,

I grasped the touch of Your voice,
Your hold when I am falling,
In deepest darkest valley I rejoice,
a hope in darkness recalling,

For sure when this dust paved road ends,
Your name and mine, they will survive,
Past the vale of shadows I will be home again,
The evening sky beckons, stars alive.

I thought of you when there are doughnuts,
and happy chatter all around.

A Friend

I pray that hope comes,
on sad heartless days,
when your door is shut,
when silence falls,
when words are strangely deaf.

When you are by yourself,
in deep troubled slumber,
I pray that God be by your side,
I pray that you'll be all right.

I'll wait outside always,
till the time day steals,
I take your dream's quiet heartbeat,
keep it while I sleep.

Beautiful Friend

I thought of you when there are doughnuts,
and happy chatter all around,
Your laughter makes me want to smile,
and laugh freely at everyone,

Skies are blue, days are frolicking fun,
when you my friend are somewhere near,
life is deep and dear,
I could stop my own from saying words,
that bring me down and out,

On rough tumble days,
I could believe in myself,
On days like these,
how sweet and kind you always be,

There is none such as you,
who could be so wickedly true,
A comfort, a hand held out in the storm,

A friend.

Missing You

When silence floods the morning light,
and you were miles apart,
There's a shattering stillness,
in the places where your words used to stand,
Saying this and that, your words took shape,
Could not help myself from laughing,
when those words were said,
Then realising those times are past,
and silence floods again.

I wish I could find you somewhere here,
and life could be wonderful again,
Though I know it deep that those times are past,
Waking up from different dreams each day,
and searching in the shadows you've left behind,
You've meant me to be strong,
though now I stand alone in the dark,
There's something in the life you've left me behind,
in the silence that floods each morning light.

If we had relentless fears and shadows,
friends then provide words and things to do.

The Breaking Of The Fellowship

Past thoughts are a load too much to say,
the paths each took when friendships part today,
A distance without end so far away,
the good old fellowship of yesterday,

A timeless tale where mighty dreams breathe,
we found where the secret goblins live,
Lost travellers we were, with books of sacred leaves,
climbing always climbing up stern and steep hills,

Playing beneath huge scarecrow-like trees,
we were part of something great that exists,
Running always running, endless and carefree,
laughing always laughing, in such glorious glee!

But time took us always to someplace new,
One life to live, one never-ending journey,
If we had relentless fears and shadows,
friends then provide words and things to do,

And though we had many more miles to go,
A vast planet to explore, a sea without end,
roads that go further than the lonely heart could know,
We will always remember how this world looks,
once upon a memory.

Thank You For Being My Friend

I will miss you, my truest friend and confidante,
May your tomorrows be days full of hope, joy and courage,
In your new home, let your heart be at peace,
for your family, your loved ones, are no more to be missed,

I thank God for all the times I had with you,
No truer friend I had in my life, then feeling blue,
Who asks me not out of curiosity's sake,
the one who talks to me and really truly makes,

Me feel you're one of the only ones who deeply cares,
One of the only ones to ever think of me and dares,
to be different than others, to be always good to another,
In times of need, you were there,

When others just look at me,
and laugh themselves bare,
Thank you for giving a hand,
Thank you for being a friend.

The Hard And Horrid Truth Of Being Someone Utterly, Utterly Famous

You might think I'm lucky for the love shown in my own favour,
if it may not be for umpteenth presents and oaths sworn to me,
For the many great lengths people go to shake hands,
to take selfies when we meet,
How adoring they are, how blessed I am,
but there is no truth to the love I receive.

For if I were to switch places with any of you,
my cup will be runneth over with happiness at every turn I see,
A commoner's life is what I aspire and am won't to be,
for the love I be given is the truest truth that I reap,
and I live knowing how I'm truly loved,
Although I'm despised by status,
I am perfectly happy and forever,
as grateful as can be.

The End.

Circumstances produce something in us,
that makes us hate and grow apart.

Worry No More

I tend to worry,
about what others say,
what others think,

No matter how hard I tried,
to let it go,
it still stings,

When others look at you with such disdain,
Those friendships I tried hardest,
to put a distance,

For the hurt that they gave,
was not worth,
in the life that I live,

I told myself,
I'd be fine,
without them,

For I'd be without confines,
that which I set myself in relationships,
that entirely is,

Without any meaning,
free from being withheld,
by who I truly am,

So I worry no more,
for the things that they say,
for the things that they think,

I am free.

I Remember When The Night Sky Called Out My Name

I remember when the night grew dark and profound,
When there were no clouds about,
and I was out in the depths of the woods,
of the world that I thought,

As I walked the road home,
the felicitous wind passed by,
My whole being listened,
listened to its lonely lullaby,

Calling all who hear its lovely melody,
to go sleep,
to dream deep,

But my soul felt a familiar tug,
'The world is lovely and yet dark',
and it called to hurt me,
with its devastating beauty,

And because of whatever I held on,
it was ugly,
Bended, tattered, deeply battered,
it was ugly, ugly, ugly!

I felt the night sky calling out my name,
Asking me to let things go,
to forgive, to forgive and just let go,

But I couldn't, I couldn't,
I promise to try again another day,
Maybe when it's daylight I'll think differently,
I promise to try to let it go,

But I doubt so,
for it hurts too deep to let things go,
But I need, I need to let them go,

One day,
Soon,

Maybe.

Words Of Wisdom

Circumstances produce something in us,
that makes us hate and grow apart,
Forgiveness brings a willingness to love again,
provided that we be given the conviction,
that we won't be,

Second time fools.

For I love you like the blue of the sea,
and the deepest azure of the sky.

To Love In Doubt

To love someone is to be happy but my heart beats with doubt,
For it said for sure a certain sadness will follow me about,
and I will hurt badly when those people throw me,
words that are sharp at their edges,
words that hit me hard at heart in my rib cages,

Those people whom I love more than they will ever love,
such a person as me,
who is just a nobody,

They will hurt me raw,
they will hurt me more,
with words that show they do not care for me,
and actions that speak truer than the eye could see,

For the fear that rises in me,
will never lie low,
and it overpowers me to know,

That I love them more than they will ever love me,
That although the pain of being left behind and ignored,
left my heart feeling empty and hollowed,
like a rock that is heavy,

And maybe, I still do care for them,
Am I a person who is not fit to live well and be happy?
Give me some love or just let me be?
and really my beating heart still aches,

For me,
and me alone,
For if maybe I could learn to love myself more,
and leave them out the door,

All would be good,
All would be well,
and dreams could come true,

Until a day comes when there's,
someone who could love me as I am,
Someone who would love me as I love him,
My heart would be perfect and whole again,

And my nightmares would be gone.

For I Love You Like The Bird That Is Free

When past events move me to pause and think,
I twist and turn, the night grew worn and old,
I couldn't sleep a wink,

For the world is coloured in washes and shades of blue,
and the darkest black that enfolds me,
calling me deep my name to sleep,
I'm drowning for I can never stop,
contemplating of the what have been's and what if's,

Then at last I close my eyes,
Deep down my heart beats enough and true for you,
and slumber comes and nightmares grasped me,
While I falter at the edge of dreams,
walking, running, stopping…

Falling deep wondering,
if I fall and grapple for hands,
Will you come for me as a friend?
When it's obvious you're leaving me,
for reasons I couldn't comprehend,

My being is in the depths of my agony,
For I love you like the blue of the sea,
and the deepest azure of the sky,
You're like the breeze that has no home and a place to rest,
a thrush that stops by on a lonesome branch,

For I love you like a bird that is free,
and I will let you go further from me,
Away and beyond me,
Though part of my heart is gone with you,
and the one that is left lives on stronger,

And glad to be without you.

Enough

When it came to pass,
and everything I did,
never seemed to be enough,

You were just the same old self,
that I've ever known,
Since the first time
we met, where I'm
just a tool,
somebody useful,

And I tended to be happy,
with the way things were,
But because of too much weightage,
of the things that happened,
that made me think you mightn't even care,
of me as your friend,

Just caring for the things that you,
were wont to think of,
All those things of you,
those things that never included me,
in your thoughts,

So, I guess there was enough in me to feel,
that I should let,
me go,
out that door.

Goodbye.

If I could say those words,
the sigh from the heart...

When Sleep Comes Not

As night unfurls its way into our minds,
I can't help but ask surreptitiously,
Why sleep doesn't come all at once,
unless if I tire for having had errands done.

I'm always running hard to this very day,
The end its sight is to behold and envy,
Those who reach it will have exhausted their life goals,
and regret not before they die and grow old.

Oh no! Those endless thoughts what are they,
Those inherent words I think shouts back darkly,
That's when I know I couldn't for the life of me,
Figure out how to fall asleep and soundly.

My heart aches longing hard for the night to end,
but no can do and I can only twist and turn,
and beneath it all my heart remembers your face,
and my lips mouth out your name again and again.

Is This Love?

It's so uncertain to feel the way I do,
in looking at you always and not exactly know,
what really is stirring in me,
deep, dark and true,

Is it even a real feeling,
or just my morning cuppa conniving,
to make me feel butterflies in my throat,
when I speak to you I kind of choke,

Fumbling for the right words to say,
scrambling for the right things to do,
You make me think of you,
when I least expect it.

And time doesn't seem to be moving,
The seconds seem to stop,
and all I could do,
was breathe in thoughts of you,
and let your name exhale in a whisper,

From my fervent lips.

Words

Words, the shape of these words,
They stuck in my throat,
trying hard to take flight,
On its own, in my mind's eye,
they beat aimlessly around,
Words failing, falling down,
in my head, a droning scattering sound.

If I could say those words,
The sigh from the heart,
Those words,
stuck in the throat,
I could have said it,
without you around.

But what use is that,
Whenever you are near,
my heart in my throat,
Those words on my lips,
tip of my tongue.

They float in my dreams,
Woke me up,
in the bitter cold.

'I love you'.

Your words are immense, they speak true,
Your words, are love in action.

Naked

In moments that I am near you,
your voice pulls me in deep,
I am lost in that juncture, and shudder,
for your voice affects me,
grips me fully, even while I sleep.

It rendered my heart asunder,
stirred me to own the things,
that I could not bravely speak,
The darkest secret that I keep,
the aching that temptation brings.

Then it happened one day,
you were near me again,
I turned, and was truly astounded,
by your voice, insistently calling,
Your lips, sounding the shape of my name.

You rendered me speechless,
by the way you held me in your regard,
I stood on my own, bare for all to see,
I wish, I could blend in with the air I breathe,
and pray for everything I feel to finally discard,

Except you held my arm firmly,
asking, "Would you like to be friends?"
But I am broken for your eyes saw me through,
My facade lost, my full-blown feelings unfettered, free,
and I could not possibly ever pretend,

That how I felt is a thing untrue,
My soul bare naked under your gaze, unplanned,
The words that were left unsaid,
you probably knew,
as you and I shook hands,

And our history finally began.

All Those Times I Caught You Unawares

For all the uncertainties,
those overwhelming things you've said,
or sometimes not say,
The millionth times when I've shed,
tears over something so improbably mundane,

You were ever so patient,
though your exasperated looks,
when I'm feeling down and out,
It somehow held a meaning,
underneath of what's beyond my grasp,

Those moments,
I've thought of all those times back,
Turned it over in 'my pretty little head',
as you called it,
I guess I've overlooked it before,
until once in recent times,
I've caught you looking at me,

You were so unaware of how your eyes were twinkling,
oblivious to the upturn of your mouth,
when you breathe in those words I said,
"Let's get out of here",
at a gathering of friends we had,

In return, you replied, "Shall we?",
and gave me your hand,
when you pull me up in my doldrums,
just to go to a fast-food restaurant?

That speaks volumes of how much,
you liked me,
and I'd forever try in my power,
for things to remain that way,

If ever time-freezing were my power that is.

Those Ten Words

The rains came, meeting the dawn,
A pitter-patter of lovely feet,
down my dusty worn-out rooftops,
I, curl up in my lonely, pensive mood,
and try to be deeply sleeping,
dripping of world-worn dreams,
while the city awakes,

Tangled in my bed,
in my sheets and trusty blanket,
Though daybreak has passed ages ago,
I'm still somewhat half asleep,
Thinking of you and what you've said,
in the movies when you held my hand,
"Isn't it wonderful to have someone love you so deeply?"

A rumble in my tummy sets me up quickly,
I scramble out of bed reluctantly,
to make my cup of hot coffee,
Uncertainty is ripping me apart,
between a toast or my maggi mee,
I settle for my fave instant noodles,
although it is a wee bit unhealthy,

I truly love these mornings,
especially when it rains during my days off,
and I am away from taxing, tiring work,
A ping comes in from my phone,
a roiling uneasy feeling for the incoming text,
but fierce starlight reflected in my being,
when I saw it was only from you,

Your words helped me get through tough times,
Your words are the sunlight that shines in angles,
through my heart's dreary window panes,
enormously lighting up wherever I am in,
Your words are immense, they speak true,
Your words, are love in action,

"Would you be free this afternoon?
Let's meet up!" and I smiling,
like the fool that I was, answered "OK!
Let's", and "What are you doing?"
You, echoed the thoughts in my soul,
when your reply pinged in,
"Nothing.
Just missing you."

And I, thinking of the shade of your eyes,
when you uttered those ten words,
Looking at me with the smile that stirs me inward,
Thinking again of what you've said yesterday,
when you held my hand, clutching it to your heart,
"Isn't it wonderful to have someone love you so deeply?"
Those words, they struck me senseless,

They changed me,
to the point,

Of no return.

That certain smile of yours,
that radiate the soul of my heart.

Something In Me That I Would Never Let Go

Thinking nothing means everything to me now,
for thoughts abound everywhere,
thoughts of you,
sitting in that chair,

Like weeds begging to be plucked,
thoughts of you smiling,
saying something to me,
but doing something else, I didn't hear,

That one moment passed,
and after that,
when I, walking through doors,
surviving and living in a reality,
that has no longer you with me,

I forgot,
To my regret, I forgot.

I forgot in every daydreams,
when I'm overwhelmed in trying to catch up,
with what you said,
back in that one moment,
You holding my hand,
trying to distract me from doing what I did,

Cutting up cucumbers,
for our sandwiches,
and in every waking moments,
that I seem to hear you,
which I did not,
and feel you,

In the faint fingerprints,
I imagined you pressed upon my arms,
Urgently whispering those words,
that I sadly,
did not hear,

That day though,
when you were no more,
and at which tears fell like forever,
no matter where I see,

Tears fell bitterly,
no matter where I am,
when thoughts of you,
intrude,

And I am in agony,
only known to people who have lost,
a hope they have within,
When suddenly,
I feel those words bubble up inside me,

And though I never know where to look,
for those words you said again,
and I realised that,
although what you speak were long gone,
and carried to your grave,

But your grip, and your touch,
the eyes you forced me to look,
before I got distraught,
your bright smile,

All those things when you uttered those words,
they said everything,
echoing what my heart knew all along,
You were trying to say those words,
I truly needed most,

"I love you too".

Silence Is Your Way Of Saying Things

What do you hear when silence breathes loudly?
When you were on your deathbed,
looking inward at the things I've said,
not exactly responding,

When silence steals those words you want to express,
I hear the static air,
I hear the thunder resounding in my ribcage,
and feel my heart stumble uncertainly,
And I know somehow it might storm somewhere,
in the depths of the world that is mine,

That day, when I last held your loving face,
the empty breeze rushed by and passed,
all my questions back in return,
Those blank looks you gave me,
when I screamed out your name,
though it never left the tip of my tongue,
for I choked back my agony…

I couldn't quite comprehend,
this utter silence that stood between us,
the pang that breaks me,
when I held your cold hands,

As the darkness of the sky grows even darker outside,
for the world will weep with me,
I know now, that
silence is your way of saying things,
against the pale blue numbness of my heart,

Silence was your way of trying to say,
that you loved me,
that everything is going to be alright,
when you went out that door,
for there was a slight pressure in my left palm,
before your silence thundered in my thoughts,

For I could no longer think when,
I could no longer count your breaths,
through the heaving of your chest,
and the gentle breeze caressed,
my agonised tears,
that fell unending,

Head bowed,
fists clenched in the folds,
of the fabric of your bed, I…
sobbing endlessly,
All my questions unanswered,
left hanging in mid-air,
in the silence that you left,

A loud exclamation,
that exists in a sentence.

Why? Why? Why!

Comfort Remains In Places That We Used To Know

There is comfort in the way things remain,
how dusts settle on books,
how the light shafts from windows lit up the gloomy room,
the way this place makes me feel,

Even when there is no longer you anchoring me,
where we belong is a concept,
that is as fathomless as the theories,
in school that never works,

Those things that are no longer useful,
but yet those are what enveloped me,
with comfort as the years go by,
How familiar it is to smell these,
pages in the books that I hold,

Remembering your remarks,
on passages that you find,
caught your attention,

That certain smile of yours,
that radiate the soul of my heart,
the crinkling sound of old weather-worn sofa,
that we used to sit,

And the spot where we held hands,
your touch,
I never want to let go,
those times,

As we drank deep our laughter,
completely drunk,
in the days of our youth,

Those days,
are long gone,
Only memories of it passed by seamlessly,
In thoughts of you,
when you left me wandering aimless,

When you left your life,
and I had to go on alone, I...
holding fast to the comfort that remains,
in the places that you used to be,

Sometimes hugging myself to sleep,
trying to forget,
trying to...
forget,
and failed,

For I never did want,
to let you go.

It is a thief,
that steals my soul.

When Dreams Come

In darkness deep, in moments few,
turning time burnt lost in you,
Memories scattered as bluebirds fly,
in perfect skies stark bright and true,

I do not know how dreams breathe,
in heavens that are as vast,
as the oceans underneath,
for those filled up with thoughts of you,

For a dream is made of lava and fire,
dust and ashes,
It is a thief,
that steals my soul,

On Earth where shadows have grown dim,
those dreams are made from my heart,
They are made with love,
from me to you,

Perhaps in my dreams,
heartfelt and though too few,
and I, foolish that I was,
trapped as a leaf,

Could hope in my wildest hope,
To finally,
find,

You.

An Epic Romance

I sometimes keep those sunshine dreams,
in hard folds of my raging heart,
When times are right in darkest nights,
I make a wish so dear to me,
that next I see is a world I want,

Beauty in crowds that move in tandem,
kind faces and friendly voices in shops and restaurants,
Free food and books for everyone,
family and true friends in abundance,

Peace, harmony, and love aplenty,
The world I know I want,
is a city of dreams that live inside of me,
an epic romance that speaks loudly,

I hold them in both my fists tightly,
when I'm awake or half asleep,
My heart a stormy, stubborn sea,
an epic romance that is in me,

Though now my dream-world only exists,
in failed fantasies, for I am one and alone,
Though try as much I might,
I can only conjure my own romance,
and only control what is mine,

So I wish for others to do the same,
and realise their own epic romance,
For each one of us makes the world,
Beautiful as a perfect pearl.

What My Dreams Are Made Of

The dreams I always have,
are breaths of life,
taken in shock fulls,
as one would,
after almost drowning.

Not charcoaled embers of time,
held by,
chained and restrained,
stamped upon,
dead.

Those fervent dreams,
fierce and ardent,
They are on wings,
of burning fire,
on ice.

They burnt my heart cold,
when I ignore their call,
Those dratted dreams,
burnt me,
burnt me with an ache,

When I do,
completely,

Nothing.

For you were just a shadow that I dreamed about.

It Was But A Shadow Of Words I Thought

I scribbled those words that I had in me,
It was but a shadow of the worlds I caught,
myself thinking of things and people,
in those far-flung off places,
that I dreamed about,

Whereof I went missing in my reverie,
of daylights that I've lost,
myself,
completely,
in dreams of you,

And you alone,
calling me up,
in my wakefulness of plenty,
during nights that I couldn't sleep,
but you,

You were just a shadow of the words,
that I thought of,
when I tried to write you down,
The way those times with you,
how it made me feel,

How it made me,
me.

But I failed.

For you were just a shadow that I dreamed about.

What Is In Me I Use Them To Write Myself Out

When it moves me, I write,
pages upon pages,
of words that I do not know,
whence it came from,

But deep inward I poured it forth,
I wrote standing in and out,
turned myself inside out,

For it is in my blood,
as others that came before me,
those who wrote,
in the mid of nights,
and the bleakest part of the day,

To use my vein as the link,
blood as the ink,
bone as the setting,
to set my words for all eternity,

And the soul that possessed me,
as the instrument that moves my pen,
and the end result that comes,
is more than a dream,

More than I ever could behold,
for the stories that I birthed,
might live longer,
than I myself ever will,

Though it is the blood and my bone,
and the core of my soul,
Those words dripping in those pages,
are what you read,
and hold in your hands now.

Words live longer than I ever will.

Love books well,
and they will love you well.

In The Pages Of The World Only Known To Bookworms

I love the worlds folded in the gentle pages of my books,
for when I breathe in those plain type fonts I see,
It's deeper than the deep of my thoughts,
bottomless than any phantom seas that are conceived,

My breath caught at a passage,
and my eyes followed the trails of those words I read,
those words I grasp at my right palm's edge,
and fell and felt,
enthralled in my tiptoes of dreams I bought,

For I am in the world unbeknownst to all,
but to those whose books they adore,
the pages of worlds that only bookworms know,
a secret world that I keep,

A part of me that I call,
I call my own.

If I could care to enter,
there would no longer be plain old me,
a girl who struggles at every turn,
without any good outcome in return,

In my place there'd be someone,
stronger, better, wiser,
someone who gets to triumph at all odds,
someone who could finally be content,

For she would conquer,
and overcome the many trials,
and be at peace with the world,

So when I'm back to where I am,
I tried to take some of those values,
and feel of those worlds,

But try as I might,
only its echoes bare remain,
And I continue my search in the dim of the light,
in the bleakest dark of the night,

Believing I'm still undefeated.

An Ode To Books

All those dusty, burdened tomes you see?
On shelves at good old libraries,
All those lovely gems at stores I hold,
ended last my room with me.

All those complex words everywhere,
made me laugh and learn, and curse,
I polish its edges I will feel,
its deepest core, pure simplicity.

Hardened me to hopes I know,
when alas a love I love painfully dies,
And impaled my heart when taken away,
the breath I hold in when I read.

Its end I could not perceive,
gripped me in my battle seat,
shocked me to a silence complete,
speaks louder than any memory.

All those tales that I am in,
greater than any I conjure,
Other things so mundane,
pales sorely to this in contrast.

Fairy tales and adventures,
wars, history and poetry,
A world beyond that I reach,
when I choose a book to read.

Love books well,
and they will love you well,
Pick a book, and you'll find a friend,
One so true, till the end.

He keeps me safe when darkness comes.

There Is No One In This World Like My Papa

There is no one in this world who could be like my papa,
He is patient, kind and loving,
He knows my worries and my fears,
the cares of my world,
my needs, my aims, my wants.

He keeps me safe when darkness comes,
at nights when I could not sleep,
He is my hero, he is there,
to hold and soothe me,
Big, strong and brave,
he is there.

There is no one in this world like my papa,
Who else but he who is wise beyond all knowledge,
Who knows what is best for me,
Who means the well of me,
There is no one who could be my papa,
except the one who already is.

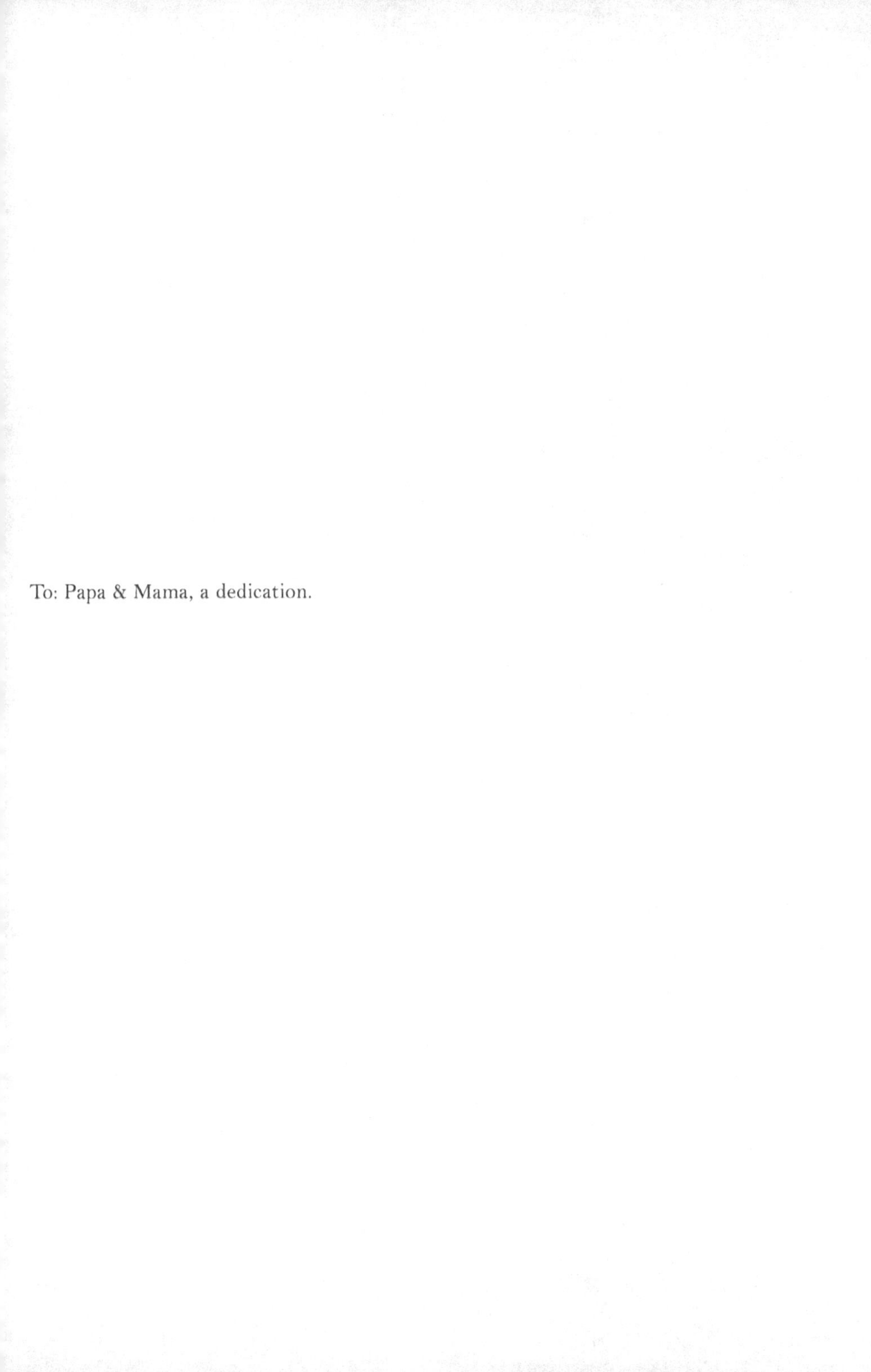

To: Papa & Mama, a dedication.

Papa

Dear Papa,

You're the love of my life,
the heart of my soul,
the reason of my being,
For without you I am lost,
but with you I am found.

I love you.

Mama

Dearest Mama,

I love you with my life,
for you did what others could not,
You're the driving force of my wellbeing,
my motivation when life gets hard,
my inspiration when all is lost,
and the extension of my soul when all is saved.

I love you.

Clouds (A Haiku Series)

Dark clouds

When dark clouds appear,
All I want are friendly rains,
But a strange storm came.

Dark clouds 2

Dark clouds hurtling by,
Showing sketches in the sky,
Winds storm and thunder.

Lost cloud

A cloud in the sky,
Unassuming, lost and dry,
It wandered and died.

On and on I struggle and still,
'All those things not ever enough'.

A Note To Remain True To Oneself Till The End Of Time

Stark raving mad her sadness,
at having to please and oblige others,
In matters of wanting to do,
in wanting to write,
or be an author,
It's absurd to think of another,
Let no one ask their neighbour,

"I want to hear the words breathe,
Their breath here my soul to live,
Further on than where it should,
Let my ink flow till I feel no more",
Dusky skies peek out the door,
Shadows wane past evening tide,
"Darkness floods and still I write",

Coughed up words from inky pens,
Quickened pace and black clouds dense,
Deep grey skies when rain comes by,
Thunder storms and sleep comes not,
All those dark, jumbled, twisted thoughts,
On and on I struggle and still,
'All those things not ever enough',

To remain true till the end of time,
she wrote when others duly scoff,
and laughingly then, walk off,
Hot-headed stubborn indulgence,
she does it with great compulsion,
Not having anything to say,
she just does things her very own way,

A ploy to keep her life less insane,
a will of iron sorely deigned,
Not bent by weather or any other being,
to remain true, to have been,
her very self, forever living,
happily ever after,
writing forever,

Till the end.

Where we hide in this lonely world,
Should we hope to meet again?

The World Is A Dark And Lovely Place 2

The world is a dark and lovely place,
in the quiet of a slumbering night,
I shall lie down dreaming....
dreaming in the open green,

When night dreams start breathing on their own,
Shall I fade from where I sleep,
and go with a heartfelt song,
to a land where stars play and hide,
in lovely meadows all aglow,

Perhaps one could know where others are,
if we look at skies and read the stars,
Where we hide in this lonely world,
Should we hope to meet again?

When silence falls on a sleepy night,
the world is a dark and lovely place.

ABOUT THE POEMS

The World Is A Dark And Lovely Place is the titular poem of this book. I had the idea to write this poem after writing *The Old Oak Tree.*

The Old Oak Tree was my first poem. It is heavily influenced by British literature because I spent my childhood reading Enid Blyton books, hence the apple trees and the said old oak tree.

The Rainbow's End was written because I believe that there is an end to rainbows. I dedicate my life to finding them.

Rain exists because I love rainy days.

Untitled was inspired by the haiku form. If you notice, each stanza has the actual 5-7-5 haiku form and because I was actually crazy about clouds that time, I wrote three Cloud haikus which I also included in this poetry collection.

My Little Butterfly was written because my nephew is such an energetic person, but I dramatised this a little bit.

Drowning is about my fear of drowning. I still carry this fear up to this day. I don't swim, so if there is a tsunami or any water disaster happening right up my alley, my only weapon is for God to protect me.

A Memory is about a girl who was so afraid to be too far out in the ocean and her brother who was so brave to keep swimming further on until the girl woke up alone on the shore. This was a nightmare I had about myself and my brother. It traumatised me, hence I had to write it out.

The Hearkened Heart is about a girl who was feeling down for many months (moons) because she'd lost the people or friends or a setting that she was so familiar with and got thrown into a new situation, she withdrew herself until someone (The Unbreaker, a friend) helped her by breaking down the door for her to move on to a new phase of her life.

A Thousand More Miles To Go, Trust Not Your Broken Heart and **On My Way Home** were written in dedication to God.

A Friend was written when I was so worried about my housemate because she did not come out of her room the whole day. Therefore, I knew she hadn't eaten or had eaten only biscuits. I felt that she was gloomy about something; I felt so frustrated that I couldn't help her. My words are deaf; meaning, my words couldn't be heard by her.

Beautiful Friend is a poem dedicated to all my true friends.

Missing You is about those times when I was alone and missing some or certain friends of mine.

The Breaking Of The Fellowship is about friendships that have to be apart because each person has their own destiny and things to achieve so they go their own ways.

Thank You For Being My Friend was written in dedication to my colleague who got a transfer to another working place.

The Hard And Horrid Truth Of Being Someone Utterly, Utterly Famous is something that I imagined a celebrity would feel. I think it's hard to find true friends if you're someone famous or rich, and that is such a sad thing.

Worry No More is something that I felt on the day I wrote it.

I Remember When The Night Sky Called Out My Name was written because I was so worried I couldn't forgive some people. I'm still trying and somehow have found a certain measure of success in finding forgiveness. Thank God.

Words Of Wisdom is a note for me to be careful in matters of the heart. I can be trusting but yet, I need to be careful in guarding my heart so that I would not be a 'second time fool'.

To Love In Doubt was lent to a friend to be posted on his Instagram. At that time, it did not have a title, and my friend titled it *Love Is A Thing You Fear*. Since this poem is 100% mine except the title, I decided to take it back and give it a new title, with a couple of changes like adding a new stanza. He did not give me a single credit for it when he posted on his Instagram, but this was a long story that happened between the two of us and I don't blame him because I somehow allowed this to happen due to me being so naive.

For I Love You Like The Bird That Is Free was written with the topic of heartbreak in mind.

Enough is again something that I felt on the day I wrote it.

When Sleep Comes Not and **Is This Love?** were written with the topic of love in mind.

Words and **Naked** were written because I think everyone, at least once had been in this situation.

All Those Times I Caught You Unawares and **Those Ten Words**
were written with a YA novel in mind.

Something In Me That I Would Never Let Go was inspired from a
scene in the movie, *Wonder Woman* when Diana the princess of Amazon
had a hearing deficiency during her fight with Ares, and Steve Trevor
was trying to tell her that he loved her before he sacrificed himself to
save the world.

Silence Is Your Way Of Saying Things was written because I will
be devastated if a loved one passed on. My paranoia was too real that I
had to write this one out.

Comfort Remains In Places That We Used To Know exists because
I feel that I find comfort in very familiar things or situations when
something bad happens.

When Dreams Come is about a dream I had about time-travelling to
find a loved one, but I somehow couldn't quite capture it in this poem.

An Epic Romance was inspired by a thought that if everyone did carry
out their purpose in life, the world would be a much, much better place
to live in.

What My Dreams Are Made Of is about my fear of forever being
mediocre and not fulfilling my life's purpose.

It Was But A Shadow Of Words I Thought is about me trying to
describe a person who means a lot to me, but failing because words fail
me.

What Is In Me I Use Them To Write Myself Out is about my love of writing, specifically poetry writing.

In The Pages Of The World Only Known To Bookworms and **An Ode to Books** are about my love for books.

There Is No One In This World Like My Papa was written because my father is everything to me.

Papa and **Mama** are poems dedicated to both my dearest parents.

Dark Clouds, **Dark Clouds 2** and **Lost Cloud** were written when I was going through a phase of haiku obsession.

A Note To Remain True To Oneself Till The End Of Time was written because at its very core, I knew that my purpose in life is to write and get published, so to hell with naysayers.

The World Is A Dark And Lovely Place 2 is an apt conclusion about whether we will find each other again, especially our loved ones and friends or relatives whom we hold dear once the world is no more.

ACKNOWLEDGEMENTS

The Rainbow's End has appeared in *The Star* newspaper on 9th January 2008.

Rain has appeared in *The Star* newspaper on 16th July 2008.

I WOULD LIKE TO THANK

God, my Father in Heaven and the Lord Jesus Christ for being with me in this journey of writing my poetry book.

My papa and mama, for loving and caring for me.

Both my brothers, Benjamin Chu Min Xian and Peter Chu Min Jian for being the best brothers a girl could ever have.

All my true friends, especially

Hor Foong Yee, my precious and dearest friend from Singapore,

Asvini Krishnamuthi, my kindest and loveliest friend who is ever so patient with me,

Annette Rowena A Marian Anthony, my bookish friend and someone I look up to,

Brenda Magdeline Robson and Judy Chong, both of whom taught me the ways of the world in matters of the heart and other whatnots,

Satthiya Kandi, my fellow poet and bookish friend,

Nurul Afifah Noor Azmi, a friend whom I hold close to my heart,

Si Nie Yan, my best friend since my university days,

and also, all my friends from Book Huggers bookclub at JB and from KLBAC (Kuala Lumpur Book Appreciation Club).

All my relatives for the care throughout all the years I was growing up.

All the students, teachers, staff members and workers at SMK Puteri Wangsa, Ulu Tiram for making me the person I am today.

Nickey Teoh from The Inspiration Hub, whom I always messaged on Whatsapp in the early wee hours of the morning, thank you for being so patient with me; the editor, JK Lee who edited this work of mine with such meticulous detail and the designer, Justin Wong who did a good job on the book design; everyone on the team who made this book a physical reality.

To all these people, I owe you guys the deepest, sincerest thanks.

Thank you,
Carol Meiyin

THE AUTHOR

127

The author is a high school teacher teaching English in the southern state of Johor, Malaysia which is very near to the island country of Singapore. During her free time, she reads and writes poetry. She is a self-confessed coffee addict who loves rainy days. Sometimes she does reviews for books, crochets (obsessively) and plays the piano.

For more of her adventures, you can follow her on Instagram at www.instagram.com/carol_meiyin